The Girl
Who Loved Pots

Rosilyn Seay

To Robert, Nathanael, and Kevin for their continuous and unwavering support in the creation and production of this book.
To Vanessa, Muriel, Kai, and Jennifer for providing essential feedback during the early stages of this book.
To the memories of my original support system (Corrine, Leroy, Fredia, Lelia, and Jackie) for whose love and influence I am eternally thankful.

Library of Congress Control Number: 2017940316

978-0-9985576-0-1

Printed and Bound in the United States of America
PicBooks Publishing
http://picbookspub.com

CONTENTS

May's Favorite Things

For as long as she could remember, May had loved pots. It didn't matter if they were big or little, round or flat, colored, black, or gray. It didn't even matter if they were for boiling, baking, or frying. May just loved all the pots in her mother's kitchen.

May didn't cook with the pots. In fact, she wasn't allowed to touch hot pots or go near the stove. Still, she did have May sized oven mitts. Those she used for make believe boxing and karate. The pots, well, they could be used for make believe everything else.

Naturally, May had other favorite things besides boxing, karate, and pots. Without a doubt, her most special thing in the world was spending time with her mother in their apartment. They would sit, talk, and share secrets. Though May always seemed to do most of the talking.

She also loved Sunshine, her blue bunny. Sunshine had been around forever and was now a little worn. His song, "You Are My Sunshine", no longer played. But when May was sad or couldn't sleep, she would still squeeze him and hug him tight. Sometimes she would sing the sunshine song herself.

Now there was only so much May could do with Sunshine, or any of her other toys. That's why she liked pots. They could be used for almost anything. Take the round ones. Her mother used them for making things like spaghetti and boiling hotdogs. But, for May, they were perfect for drumming.

Then there were the flat ones that May's mother called cookie sheets. Her mother used those to make things like buns, biscuits, and pizzas. Best of all she used them to make May's favorite snack, chocolate chip cookies. But to May and Bear, they made perfect table tops for their tea parties.

Of all the pots, her favorites were those that fit on her head. She would wear them and march like she imagined her father, the soldier, did. Sometimes she'd sing along as she marched. Now and then she'd pretend to be one the ants from the counting song, "Ants Go Marching".

But of all her favorite things, her most favorite was that her parents didn't mind that she loved pots. They even kept them within her reach, in the bottom of the cupboard. So whenever she wanted to, May could play and have as many pretend adventures as she could think up.

Miss Josephine

Then one day May's mother had to leave her with Miss Josephine, the new babysitter. To May, she seemed awfully big and a bit scary. Even her purple bag was almost as big as May. Looking up, May asked her, "Are you a giant?"
Miss Josephine laughed as she answered, "No dear. I'm not."

May tried, but she couldn't take her eyes off of the big purple
bag. Pointing to it, she asked, "What's that?"

Miss Josephine smiled and said, "This is my smart bag."

May was stumped. She didn't know what to think about a giant
who wasn't really a giant carrying a bag that was smart.

At the door, May wouldn't let her mother go. Even when her mother tried to soothe her, May held on tight.

Finally, Miss Josephine reached for her and said, "Believe it or not, dear, I have a feeling that we will be great friends."

May didn't really believe it. But she did let go.

The Smart Bag

Later, as Miss Josephine unpacked her smart bag, May couldn't believe her eyes. Everything in it looked like school stuff. She asked, "Why can't I play with my own toys?"
"Trust me," Miss Josephine answered. "You'll enjoy the things from my smart bag just as much."
Since she had no choice, May just said, "Ok."

Still she was curious. May had never heard of a smart bag before. So finally she asked, "Why is your bag smart?"

Miss Josephine laughed. "The bag is just a bag," she said. "But the books, blocks, puzzles, and games in it make you think. Anything that makes you think helps make you smarter."

"Really?" thought May. She knew that getting smarter was a good thing. She just never realized it was quite that easy. Now she wondered, "If playing with blocks and puzzles make you smart, what about playing with pots?"
But she decided to keep that question to herself.

May's Big Idea

With all that reading, building, and thinking, May got really tired. When she couldn't hold out any longer, she did something that she hardly ever did. She asked if she could take a nap. And when she returned from her nap, May was surprised to see that Miss Josephine had needed a nap too.

So, May decided to play quietly on her own. The first thing she did was put together a big puzzle.

Then she tried stacking blocks. But it wasn't as much fun if you couldn't crash them. Crashing the blocks would make too much noise.

Finally, she tried reading one of Miss Josephine's books.

Then it hit her. Her best idea yet. She wondered why she had not thought of it before. This was perfect. Since Miss Josephine was fast asleep, May could explore the pots in the kitchen. Miss Josephine would never know.

Trying not to disturb Miss Josephine, May tiptoed to the kitchen. Right away she found a red pot she had never seen before. "Great," she whispered, "I love red!"

She eased it onto her head. Excited, she was just starting to march, when from the living room she heard, "May! Where are you?"

No way was she going to get caught with her mother's pot on her head. So she tried to pull it off, but it wouldn't budge. She tugged and tugged. Still, it wouldn't come off. "Maybe I should just hide," she thought.

But it was too late. Miss Josephine had found her.

May started crying. She was sure she was in big trouble. Then, pointing to the pot, she said, "It's stuck. It won't come off!" The closer Miss Josephine got, the harder she cried.

"I do like your smart stuff," May sobbed. "But I like pots too. Even if they don't make me smart."

"Oh my. You poor thing," Miss Josephine said softly. She paused to think for a moment. Then she did something May never expected. She bent down and pulled her close. She hugged May tight like that, until she was totally calm. Then Miss Josephine slowly and carefully lifted the pot off of May's head.

Really Great Friends

Miss Josephine then took the red pot to wash it with the morning dishes. May watched. She could not believe that Miss Josephine didn't seem upset. After all, she had caught May with a pot stuck on her head.

Overjoyed, May just talked about everything, even her adventures with pots.

"My goodness, such imagination," Miss Josephine said.

May got quiet. She had heard that word a lot. She wasn't sure if it was good or bad. So, she asked, "Does imagination make you smarter?"

Miss Josephine sat down. Then she gave May's hand a gentle squeeze before answering. "Yes," she said, "most definitely!"

Miss Josephine then got up to put away the pots and dishes. She seemed to be thinking about something. Finally, she bent down and took out two big pots and four big spoons from the cupboard. Sitting on her knees, she placed the pots upside down on the floor between them.

May looked on, shocked. She couldn't believe it when Miss Josephine started banging on the pots like drums. Beating out a rhythm, Miss Josephine said, "You know what May? I sort of like pots too. But maybe it's safer to beat them than to wear them."

Laughing out loud, May ran over and gave Miss Josephine a really big hug.

Later, as she was leaving, Miss Josephine bent down to May's level. She whispered, "Next time, you can teach me more about playing with pots."

Then she laughed and said, "But I think I'll add a May sized apron to my smart bag. That way I can teach you how to share in washing the pots."

May giggled. She had to admit that Miss Josephine had been right. They had become really great friends.

CPSIA information can be obtained
at www.ICGtesting.com
Printed in the USA
LVHW07*1505150518
577259LV00025B/464/P